For Hannah, a wicked story for my WICKED niece! – M. S.

For Rosa & Eliana – D. T.

BLOOMSBURY CHILDREN'S BOOKS
Bloomsbury Publishing Plc
50 Bedford Square, London, WC1B 3DP, UK

BLOOMSBURY, BLOOMSBURY CHILDREN'S BOOKS and the Diana logo are trademarks of Bloomsbury Publishing Plc

First published in Great Britain by Bloomsbury Publishing Plc

Text copyright © Mark Sperring 2019
Illustrations copyright © David Tazzyman 2019

Mark Sperring and David Tazzyman have asserted their rights under the Copyright, Designs and Patents Act, 1988,
to be identified as the Author and Illustrator of this work

A catalogue record for this book is available from the British Library

ISBN 978 1 4088 9779 9 (HB)
ISBN 978 1 4088 9778 2 (PB)
ISBN 978 1 4088 9780 5 (eBook)

1 3 5 7 9 10 8 6 4 2

Printed and bound in China by Leo Paper Products, Heshan, Guangdong

All papers used by Bloomsbury Publishing Plc are natural, recyclable products from wood grown in well managed forests.
The manufacturing processes conform to the environmental regulations of the country of origin.

To find out more about our authors and books visit www.bloomsbury.com and sign up for our newsletters

The ASTRO Naughty NAUGHTY Baddies

Mark Sperring   David Tazzyman

BLOOMSBURY
CHILDREN'S BOOKS
LONDON OXFORD NEW YORK NEW DELHI SYDNEY

Once there were FOUR
   Naughty Naughty Baddies.

One   Two

Three

Four.

And each one was as naughty as the next.

One mischief-making morning,
the Naughty Naughty Baddies were creeping about –

Creep   Creep   Creep

– when they spotted something that made them come to
a sudden excited STOP.

The Naughty Naughty Baddies gave WICKED grins and,
quick as a flash, a madcap plan formed in their villainous heads.

"We could JUMP on our spacehoppers," said One.

Boing

Boing

Boing!

"Then CLIMB into
our Badmobile,"
suggested Two.

WHOOSH!

STEAL a space rocket, thought Three.

Then BLAST OFF
at SUPER-NAUGHTY speed
all the way to the MOON.

KER-ZOOM!

The last and final part of their DIABOLICAL plan involved capturing

some aliens and claiming the FANTABULOUS reward!

But, "Hmmm," said **Four**, just as they were about to boing
into action. "That doesn't seem quite NAUGHTY enough."
Then **Four** arched a FIENDISH eyebrow and gave a WICKED laugh.

Mwa-ha-ha!

For, suddenly, **Four** had come up with the
NAUGHTIEST plan in the **entire universe**
and, best of all, it was BRILLIANTLY bonkers.

"We should SNAFFLE some knitting needles . . .

SWIPE some wool . . .

And make some gloriously GREEN alien costumes."

"Then
we should
DISAPPEAR
down a
drain...

CLIMB UP
the palace
wall...

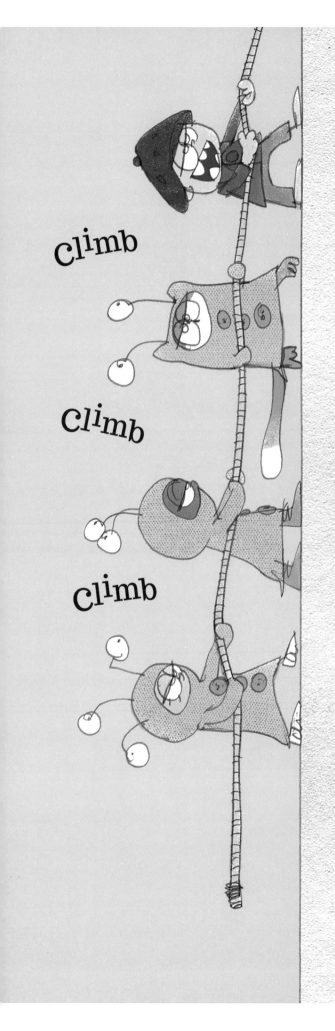

Climb

Climb

Climb

And HOODWINK
the President with our
MIND-BOGGLING
disguises!"

In three clicks of a knitting needle the DASTARDLY plan was underway and, at EXACTLY four minutes past snack time, the Naughty Naughty Baddies landed in the President's bedroom.

"Are you sure these are REAL aliens?" frowned the President. "Because Mister Snuggle-Hugs here thinks they look slightly HOMEMADE."

"Of course they're REAL," said Four. "They even have weird woolly tentacles – LOOK!"

The three green-buttoned aliens

WIGGLED and JIGGLED

their weird woolly tentacles with EXTRATERRESTRIAL glee.

Tee-hee!

What Naughty
Naughty
ALIENS!

"Well," gasped the President, after giving it some weird woolly thought,

The
President
led them
DOWN to

the deep dark depths of the presidential palace where

"I suppose these creatures do look totally OUT OF THIS WORLD.
Follow me . . ."

he revealed the most FANTABULOUS reward ever . . .

More TOYS than the Naughty Naughty Baddies had seen in their WHOLE.

VILLAINOUS.

LIVES.

It was the moment our FOUR fiendish fraudsters had been waiting for.

Yippee!

Well those Naughty Naughty Baddies
couldn't help themselves.

Grab

Grab

Grab.

One grabbed some
roller skates.

CRASH!

Two grabbed a chemistry set . . .

KABoOm!

But, oh dear, **Three** grabbed something

that THREE should NOT have grabbed . . .

Some DANGLING threads!

Whirl

Twirl

Whirly-Whirl!

Suddenly the Naughty Naughty Baddies' brilliant plan began to unravel
right before their very eyes, until . . .

OOPS!
They were completely
UNDONE!

"**FAKES!**" shrieked the President. "**FAKE** aliens! Mister Snuggle-Hugs was **RIGHT** all along."

Then, without further ado, the President announced a truly TERRIBLE punishment for those Naughty Naughty Baddies . . .

"You shall put back ALL the toys EXACTLY as you found them," he scowled. "And go home totally REWARDLESS!"

DRAT and DOUBLE DRAT!

The Naughty Naughty Baddies HATE tidying up and losing out.

But to everyone's **shock** and SURPRISE,
the Naughty Naughty Baddies **DID** put away
the President's toys, though it took them
a long **GRUMBLY** time.

Moan

Groan

Moanie-GROAN!

But they didn't go home
COMPLETELY empty-handed,
for just as the President was getting
ready for bed, a LOUD weeping wail
rang through the night . . .

"BOO-HOO!
Where's my SWEET, SWEET
Mister Snuggle-Hugs?"
came the panicked cry.
"I just CAN'T sleep
without him!"

Oh, MY! What Naughty Naughty Baddies!